THE CRIMEBUSTERS INVESTIGATE

Mark Fowler

Illustrated by Ann Johns

Designed by Lucy Parris

Edited by Corinne Stockley and Michelle Bates

Series Editor: Gaby Waters

Contents

About this book

The Crimebusters Investigate is an exciting tale of mystery and detection. Throughout the book, you are plunged into tricky puzzles which you must solve to make sense of the story. There are clues to help you on page 43, and you can check all the answers on pages 44 to 48.

A Summer Job

Kaz Smiley was not having a good summer. Somehow or other, she'd agreed to work mornings at Grimebusters, her Aunt Mary's cleaning business.

"The extra money's great," she told her friend Matt, "but I can think of at least five hundred things I'd rather be doing this summer!"

One hot, sticky Wednesday, Kaz drifted into the Grimebusters office, hoping that for once there wouldn't be too many jobs lined up for her. She pulled a note from the notice board…

…and then wished she hadn't. It looked like today was going to be a *bad* day.

If there's dirty work around call
GRIMEBUSTERS
Quick and efficient service
234 - 487 - 34

Wed August 4

Dear Kaz,
Called away on urgent personal business. Back next week. Busy morning for you, I'm afraid!
1. Scrub houseboat Aurora at Orlando Wharf until shipshape.
2. Shampoo Mrs. Turnbull's carpets with Wandascrub Suds.
3. Sweep chimneys at 124 Wharf Road.
4. Deliver leaflets from box 5.
Please lock up carefully.
Aunt Mary

Grimebuster!

Kaz gulped and read the note again. If she got all that done in one morning it really *would* be a miracle. Still, at least then she could have a couple of days off.

Weighed down by buckets, mops, brooms, vacuum cleaners and assorted bottles, Kaz staggered out to the van and set off for Orlando Wharf.

Watch out! Every single leaflet that we delivered in July had a misprint! DO NOT deliver any more leaflets from box 4.
Mary

When she arrived, she spotted the Aurora at once...

...and got to work.

First she scrubbed the portholes...

...then she swabbed the decks...

...and polished the ship's wheel.

4

At last the houseboat was clean, but there were two more calls to make…

…and a whole box of leaflets to deliver.

Amazingly, Kaz made it back to the Grimebusters office by 12:20 – with ten minutes to spare before the end of her morning.

Exhausted, she collapsed onto a pile of old boxes for a quick snooze. But a few minutes later, her peace was shattered…

Marvello Mansion

I need your help… a terrible mess… please come right away – Marvello Mansion, Morello Road…

Prrrring! The Grimebusters telephone began to ring. As soon as Kaz answered, a shrill, ear-piercing voice launched into a long speech, summoning her to a place called Marvello Mansion.

It all sounded very dramatic, but could a cleaning job really be *that* urgent?

Well – only one way to find out, thought Kaz. She grabbed a city map and set off. Half an hour and six wrong turns later, she finally found Morello Road. It was in a part of Allegro she had never been to before.

Marvello Mansion certainly looked like a real mansion. Nervously, Kaz swallowed hard and started up the path toward the marble doorway.

Before she got there, the door was flung open by a large, well-dressed woman. She seemed very flustered, and also a bit surprised.

"You're a lot younger than I'd expected," she said in her shrill voice. "But I'm sure you know your job. I'm Constanza Smith – the opera singer," she added. "No doubt you've heard of me."

And with these words, she pushed Kaz through the door.

Constanza led Kaz into a large drawing room where a strange collection of people crowded around her, all jabbering at once, and very loudly. The room was a total mess, but no one even *mentioned* cleaning.

As she listened, Kaz got more and more confused, but then she remembered Aunt Mary's note on the office door. Maybe she hadn't been called in as a cleaner at all.

What do you think?

7

^CGrimebusters!

You simply *must* find it for me. I couldn't *possibly* call in the police.

These people thought Kaz was a detective – a Crimebuster, not a Grimebuster! And they wanted her to find a stolen medallion, the Traitor's Knot.

Kaz opened her mouth to explain the mistake. But then she stopped. Being a detective would be much more exciting than cleaning carpets, she thought. She'd need some help …her friend Matt, of course! Trying to sound like a pro, she turned to Constanza.

"This case might be tricky," she said. "I think I'll need to call in my partner."

Matt? I'm not a cleaner any more – I'm a detective! And I'm going to need your help…

Alone in a side room, she rang Matt's number, then launched into a hurried explanation. Matt agreed to help at once.

Twenty minutes later, he was outside Marvello Mansion, armed with a notebook and trying to look the part. Kaz let him in, and the two detectives had a rapid 'private conference'.

Right, first we ask them all questions…

What kind of questions?

Well… er… about what happened, of course.

But when Constanza bustled back into the hall a few minutes later, she told them that her four guests had all left.

"Oh dear," whispered Kaz to Matt. "Not a very good start. Still, we'll just have to catch up with them later. What next?"

"Comb the scene of the crime for clues," pronounced Matt confidently.

This was all very well if you knew what you were looking for. There were all kinds of things on the floor, including some scraps from the display case and an overturned wastebasket, but nothing looked particularly promising.

Finally, though, some torn-up scraps of paper did catch Kaz's attention. Once pieced together, they revealed an interesting message.

What does it say?

Ne
devel
you pl..
yet? Meet
moring a..
make arra..
for the ha..
be at the
end

of
your road.
café at
please be
prompt.

dover

Wednesday 4th
ed to discuss late..
opments. H..
..nned fi..
me

..ve
nal swoop
tomorrow
ten to
..ments
I'll
the

THE TRAITOR'S KNOT
MEDALLION

Historic piece, thought to have once belonged
to Roger de Fey, governor of Allegro and opera patron.

On The Case

Was the torn note a clue? Kaz stuffed the pieces in her pocket, just in case. Meanwhile Matt had decided their next move. "We must figure out who the suspects are," he said.

"Well, that's not so difficult," said Kaz. "There were only five people in the house."

"Yes," added Matt excitedly, "And we know all the doors and windows were locked. We can't count Constanza – so one of her four guests must be the thief!" They asked Constanza for the four names, then hurried back to Grimebusters.

"OK, we need a case file," said Matt, looking up the names in an old phone book and ripping them out. Kaz joined in, gathering up other useful-looking papers.

But nothing seemed to help much, until Kaz began to think about the torn note in her pocket. Assuming it had been sent to one of their suspects, she could figure out the meeting place it mentioned.

Who was the note sent to?
Where is the meeting place?

Allegro City Telephone directory   p384

Malloney D 17 Salero St   484 983 03
Malloney S, 14 Opera Av   785 793 48

The four suspects
Hal Gough
  – hat and raincoat
Annabelle Lotte
  – tall, brown hair
Eduardo Jones
  – long hair, flamboyant clothes
Sally Malloney
  – short, red hair

Jones D, 67 Dockside   712 378 8
Jones E, 3 Red Lion Yard   478 398 2

THE TRAITOR'S KNOT

No one knows the origin of this strange medallion, which is now in the private collection of opera singer Constanza Smith. It is thought to date back to the eighteenth century when the corrupt governor Roger de Fey ruled the city. Indeed some have suggested that it may even have belonged to de Fey, and that it had some hidden significance for him. This has never been proved, and the real history and significance of the medallion remain a mystery.

ROGER DE FEY

THE TRAITOR'S KN

Lott A, 34 Lamp Street   558 973 9
Lotte A, 18 Plaza Julio   234 493 9

10

The Royal Fort is proud to announce a new exhibition:

TREASURES OF ALLEGRO
August 15th - 31st

The main attraction will be the Allegro Crown Jewels, the city's most famous – and valuable – treasures. Normally kept under lock and key in the vaults of the fort, the Crown Jewels have not been seen by the public for twenty years. Numerous other treasures will also be on display, including the strange Traitor's Knot medallion, on loan from a private collection. Don't miss this once-in-a-lifetime exhibition!

THE ALLEGRO CROWN JEWELS

Gough A, 34 Madero Pl	682 684 39	
Gough H, 13 Corneta Rd	323 452 78	
Gough K, 34 Opera Av	745 452 90	

CAFÉS
(Complete list)

Café Alfonso, 45 South St
The Golden Egg, 56 Tempest Rd
The Singing Kettle, 1 Opera Av
Café Superbo, 72 Fishmarket Row
Cosimo's Cosy Caff, 35 Cathedral St
The Chip & Lettuce, 5 Long St
Isabel's Café, 26 Western Av
The Grapevine, 37 Galleon Sq
Healthy Life Café, 12 Mistero St
The Greasy Pan, 64 Broad St

Healthy Life Café
12 Mistero St

ANTIQUES
(Complete list)

Curiosity Corner, 3 South St
Bygones, 41 Western Avenue
Joker's Antiques, 39 Lamp St
Junk & Clutter, 56 Broad St
Miscellany, 18 Plaza Julio

Allegro Landmarks
A. The Royal Fort
B. Orlando Wharf
C. The Market Place

Miscellany
18 Plaza Julio

Curiosity Corner
3, South St

Suspicions

It didn't take Kaz and Matt long to decide on their next move. They would go and spy on Sally Malloney's meeting at the Singing Kettle.

They met up early the next morning. Not quite as early as planned – that old alarm clock had to go, thought Kaz – but it wasn't long after ten when they got to the café. Right away, Kaz spotted Sally, deep in conversation with a companion.

Cautiously, they crept closer, hoping to hear what the two were talking about. Kaz did manage to hear a few words – and they confirmed her suspicions about Sally. This detective business was pretty easy, really.

There's nothing to worry about – the plan can't fail. Just keep your nerve.

A few minutes later, Sally Malloney jumped to her feet, said a hasty goodbye to her companion and hurried away from the café.

"Let's follow her," whispered Matt excitedly.

They shadowed her along dim alleyways, through a bustling street market and on into the busiest part of the city.

She's heading for the market.

12

Suddenly Sally slipped through a door. Kaz and Matt followed her into a crowded warehouse.

"We'll get a better view from that balcony," whispered Matt. At the top, they watched Sally meet a shifty-looking character.

Excitedly, Matt peered through his Super-Zoom Mini-Binoculars as Sally handed something over. It was a plan of some kind – with a coded message!

What does the message say?

13

Chaos!

What smokescreen? What map? Whatever Sally was up to, it sounded very strange, thought Kaz, as they followed her out of the warehouse.

"We have to find out where she goes next," said Kaz. It was a good idea, but before they'd gone far, Sally headed into a maze of streets, and vanished.

"So what now?" asked Matt.

"I don't know," replied Kaz, "but I'm starving. Let's find something to eat."

An hour later, wandering back to the van, they walked right into mayhem. In front of them the Governor's Mansion was spilling out people on all sides. It seemed to be on fire!

In the middle of dodging fire hoses, Matt suddenly stopped and pointed. Kaz followed his gaze. A fireman – sprinting *away* from the mansion. Weird. Then slowly, other things began to occur to her... a lot of smoke... and the time was 1:15! Kaz began to suspect very strongly that Sally Malloney was involved in all this.

What do you think?

Undercover Investigation

Kaz and Matt raced after the suspicious firefighter, determined to find out more…

…but he jumped into a waiting van, and sped off into the distance.

"There's something weird about this fire," said Kaz. "Maybe there are clues in the Mansion."

First they'd have to get inside. In a flash, Kaz realized she had the perfect cover. She dashed off.

I've been sent by Grimebusters, high pressure fire damage specialists.

A short while later she was back, laden with buckets, mops and her vacuum cleaner.

At the entrance to the Mansion, she had no trouble getting past the guard. She hurried inside.

Kaz wandered nervously through the rooms. Strangely, there was no sign of fire, just wisps of smoke. Then she overheard three people talking. Apparently an old city map had been stolen from a safe. Well, that confirms it, thought Kaz. A map… and a smokescreen! The case against Sally looked pretty watertight.

Unfortunately, it was about to leak. A loose page from a letter caught Kaz's eye. It seemed very suspicious – but the suspect wasn't Sally Malloney!

Who was it?

17

The Plot Thickens

An hour or so later, Kaz was bringing Matt up to date. "So now we have *two* suspects," said Matt. "But which is guilty? Sally? Or Annabelle? Or maybe they're in it together," he added.

"Well I'm sure the two *crimes* are connected," said Kaz. "It makes you wonder if there'll be more..."

"Maybe they're master criminals with a master plan!" Matt broke in, getting carried away.

"Hmmm... well maybe," said Kaz. "Tell you what – let's go and visit Annabelle at Miscellany."

...tomorrow... 10am... where do you want to meet?

But when Kaz and Matt got there, they didn't just find Annabelle – Sally and Constanza were there too. Annabelle seemed to be finishing off a phone call.

Kaz and Matt listened in as Constanza and Sally said their goodbyes. Constanza's parting words sounded very suspicious indeed. This was getting more confusing by the minute! As Sally turned to climb into her car, she looked straight at Kaz and Matt.

"She's looking at us *again*," hissed Kaz, as she and Matt beat a hasty retreat.

...so the Phantom Conspiracy will be a triumph! Everything's planned down to the last detail.

When they got back to Grimebusters, Kaz and Matt were still debating whether Sally, Annabelle and Constanza could possibly *all* be in it together.

Opening the door, Kaz stumbled over a pile of papers.

"Another load of junk mail," she groaned. But then she saw something. "Oh, no – remember all that smoke at the Governor's Mansion?" she said."We just got ourselves *another* suspect!"

Who?

EDUARDO'S THEATRICAL SUPPLIES

3 RED LION YARD

COSTUMES ~ STAGE PROPS
MAKE-UP ~ WIGS
SPECIAL EFFECTS ~ DRY IC[
SMOKE CANISTERS

CALL NOW ON
478 398 23

THE GRAPEVINE

Right next to the Royal Fort, this busy café brings you tastes from around the world. Whether you choose a full meal, or just a lunchtime snack, you can be sure of a warm welcome. Don't forget to visit our wine cellars – historic vaults which date back many centuries!

TREASURES OF ALLEGRO: *SPECIAL OFFER!*

Visit the spectacular *Treasures of Allegro* exhibition at the Royal Fort and you will automatically get free admission to any other historic building of your choice! *Treasures of Allegro*, brings together the most valuable and historic jewels in the city, with numerous loans from private collections. See the intriguing Traitor's Knot medallion, the glittering Castillo emeralds, and of course the world-famous Crown Jewels of Allegro normally kept under lock and key in the vaults. The exhibition runs from August 15th to 31st. Don't miss it!

THE PHANTOM CO[

ALLEGRO'S
Royal Oper House
IS PROUD
TO PRESENT A NE[
OPERA
STARRING
Constanza Smith

The Allegro Crown Jewels – see them at the Royal Fort!

Kidnap!

This was ridiculous! They now had reason to suspect almost everyone who was in Marvello Mansion the previous morning.

"So who do we investigate first?" asked Matt. "Sally, Annabelle, Constanza… or Eduardo and his smoke canisters?"

Before Kaz could reply, the phone rang. It was Sally Malloney. "I'm in terrible danger," she said. "Please come at once!"

What danger? And why call us, Kaz wondered. Confused, they jumped back into the van and set off for Sally's house.

When they arrived, they were startled to see that the door had been smashed open.

Nervously, they stepped inside. In front of them, the hall was in a real mess.

"What on earth has happened?" asked Matt, staring at the smashed pictures and upturned chairs.

Before they could explore further, a man appeared behind them, thrust a piece of paper into Matt's hand and then ran off again. After they'd read the note, Kaz and Matt looked at each other, amazed.

"Sally Malloney's been kidnapped!" Matt exclaimed. "We must rescue her!"

"Hmmm," said Kaz. "This is all getting a little confusing. But we'd better try and find her." Luckily, with the help of the message and Kaz's map of Allegro, they could figure out exactly where Sally had been taken.

I live next door to Miss Malloney. I saw two men dragging her out of her house. One of them dropped this note.

Grab Malloney at her house. Drive south to the end of her road. Turn right, pass one historic site, take next right. Take first left and first right by museum then first left. Hotel is on the right.

Where?

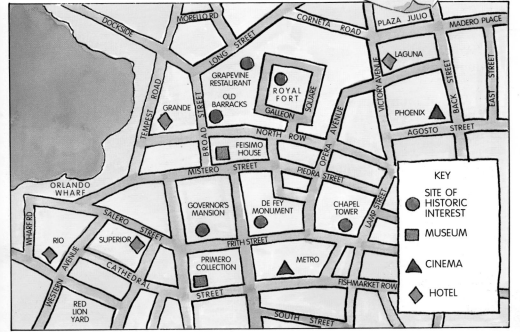

The Hotel Grande

As they made their way to the hotel, Kaz and Matt struggled to make sense of events.

"I can't understand why Sally's been kidnapped," said Matt, "but at least it means she can't be guilty of the crimes."

"I suppose not," Kaz replied. "But what about all the evidence against her? I'm totally baffled!"

It was growing dark when Kaz and Matt reached the hotel, which seemed half-derelict and run-down. "They seem very safety-conscious here," giggled Matt. "Look at all the fire escapes!" They hid behind some boxes at the back of the hotel.

"So what now?" asked Kaz. "We can't just walk in and demand to search every room."

At that moment, Matt caught a glimpse of a shadowy figure at a high window next to a flagpole. "There she is," he exclaimed. "It's Sally – up at that window."

Now they knew where they had to go. They quickly decided to climb the fire escapes and enter the room from the balcony.

Which way should they go?

We can get up there easily enough – but we'll have to climb onto the balconies as we go.

22

Rescue

Twenty minutes later, and gasping for breath, Matt and Kaz were crouching on a balcony outside the lighted room. Cautiously, they peered inside.

"There she is," hissed Kaz, pointing to a rope-bound figure in one corner. "But why is she all tied up? I thought you saw her standing at the window."

Quickly, Kaz and Matt scrambled inside and set to work on the tangle of ropes. The knots were easy enough to undo.

"Please hurry," pleaded the prisoner. "My kidnappers could return at any moment!"

As soon as she was free, they all scrambled down the precarious ladders to safety.

They ran off through the rubble behind the hotel, then collapsed in a sweaty heap next to a wall. As soon as she had her breath back, Sally Malloney launched into a long and complicated explanation of whys, whats and wheres that left little room for doubt...

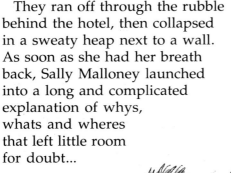

It certainly explained all those suspicious meetings and messages. Far from being the villain, Sally was actually trying to expose the criminals!

She even gave Kaz and Matt a coded note. "We think it was written by one of the Traitor's Knot thieves," she explained. "And now," she added, "I must scoot off. Thanks for everything!"

What does the note say?

Station Meeting

This gets more and more like a spy story, mused Kaz. And why didn't Sally need the note herself? "Oh well," she said, "If the Traitor's Knot thieves are going to be at the station tomorrow morning, we'd better be there too."

And so they were – along with a few hundred other people, but on time at least.

So where was the snack bar? Using a plan of the building and the coded note, they worked it out pretty quickly.

"I don't *believe* this," said Kaz, looking over at the crowded tables. "We might have cleared one suspect, but now we've gained another. Look!"

Who has she seen?

ALLEGRO STATION

BOOKS	CARDS	SNACK BAR	CHOC-OLATES	SNACK BAR	PIZZAS
SNACK BAR				NEWS	
TICKET				SNACK BAR	
PIZZAS	SNACK BAR	FLORIST	BOOKS	CHOC-OLATES	TOILETS

LOWER LEVEL

WAITING ROOM	FLORIST	TOURIST OFFICE	CHOC-OLATES	SNACK BAR	PIZZAS
CARDS				NEWS	
NEWS				PIZZAS	
PIZZAS	SNACK BAR	CHOCOLATES	FLORIST	CARDS	BOOKS

UPPER LEVEL

27

A Secret Hideout?

Annabelle Lotte – and Hal Gough! So he was mixed up in this too! Who wasn't, thought Kaz, with a sigh.

Pretty soon, the two of them got up from their table and headed through some gates.

"OK," said Kaz. "We'll follow them. We have to figure this out."

...hang on, we'll be inside in a moment...

Hal and Annabelle hurried through an engine shed to one of the office units at the back. Then Hal punched a sequence into an electronic lock.

"A secret hideout!" said Matt. "They *must* be up to something." Whatever it was, they were only inside for a few minutes before heading back into the station.

"Let's go inside and search for clues," said Matt. "Maybe we'll find some evidence against Hal and Annabelle. There's only one problem," he added, "the lock."

"Not such a problem!" said Kaz, beginning to think she was turning into an expert detective after all. "I watched Hal. The combination's 7814."

Actually, it turned out to be 8714, but it wasn't long before Kaz and Matt were inside.

Not exactly a villains' den, thought Kaz, looking around the tidy office. And after scanning a few diary pages, she was soon convinced that their two suspects weren't suspects at all...

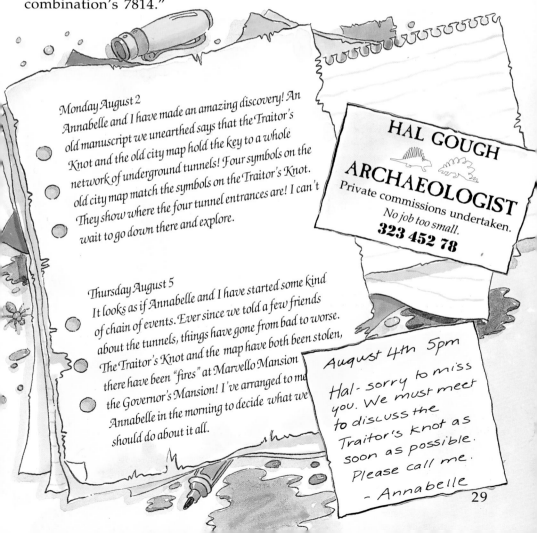

Monday August 2
Annabelle and I have made an amazing discovery! An old manuscript we unearthed says that the Traitor's Knot and the old city map hold the key to a whole network of underground tunnels! Four symbols on the old city map match the symbols on the Traitor's Knot. They show where the four tunnel entrances are! I can't wait to go down there and explore.

Thursday August 5
It looks as if Annabelle and I have started some kind of chain of events. Ever since we told a few friends about the tunnels, things have gone from bad to worse. The Traitor's Knot and the map have both been stolen, there have been "fires" at Marvello Mansion the Governor's Mansion! I've arranged to me Annabelle in the morning to decide what we should do about it all.

HAL GOUGH
ARCHAEOLOGIST
Private commissions undertaken.
No job too small.
323 452 78

August 4th 5pm
Hal - sorry to miss you. We must meet to discuss the Traitor's knot as soon as possible. Please call me.
- Annabelle

29

Strange Events

So Hal and Annabelle were innocent – just investigating a little bit of Allegro's history! But why arrange their meeting so secretly, wondered Kaz.

"The interesting thing about all this is the tunnels," said Kaz.

"Yes," agreed Matt. "Whoever stole the city map and the Traitor's Knot must have known about them – and was very eager to find out more. But why?"

Neither Matt nor Kaz had an answer to this, so they returned to their list of suspects.

"We think we can rule out Sally, Annabelle and Hal," Kaz began. "So that leaves Constanza and Eduardo Jones. I think it's time we went to Eduardo's Theatrical Supplies."

When they finally found it, Eduardo's was locked up and shuttered. Kaz and Matt crept around to the back, and almost stumbled straight into the middle of a very strange scene.

Two heavily disguised figures were letting themselves into Eduardo's back door. From something they said, Kaz guessed they were planning a crime with Eduardo.

It looks as if Mr. Jones has left the stuff ready for us. Everything we need for the operation is here.

The two men disappeared for a few moments, then re-emerged, and began loading a yellow truck with crates and boxes. Then, as Kaz and Matt crept closer, one of them pulled out a mobile phone and started to talk. Kaz and Matt strained to listen, but only caught a few words.

They did hear him mention a 'safe place' where the boxes were to be taken. And the names seemed familiar...

"I know exactly where that is!" exclaimed Kaz, suddenly.

Where is the 'safe place'?

Orlando Wharf

Clearly, Kaz and Matt had to investigate the villains' 'safe place'. They waited until the coast was clear…

…then set off for Orlando Wharf. They arrived just as the yellow truck sped off again. Now it was safe to explore the Seamist.

Cautiously, they approached the boat. They climbed onto the deck and then, finding an unlocked hatch, quickly slipped down into the main cabin. Almost at once, Matt gasped with excitement. "Look over there!" he shouted.

"The stolen map! *And* the Traitor's Knot! We've found it, Kaz!" he cried.

There it was, just sitting there. What they'd been looking for all along, and yet...

Something told Kaz this wasn't the end of the trail. Who had carried out the thefts? And why? A coded message lying next to the Traitor's Knot might help.

What does it say?

Revelations

It looked as if *another* crime was planned – some grand scheme was reaching its climax. That night, Kaz lay awake (with the Traitor's Knot and the map both safely under her pillow), going over everything in her mind.

At least they'd been right about the tunnels. They seemed to be a vital part of the plan, whatever the plan was. The coded message talked about vaults ...maybe that was important.

It was all so confusing. Who was behind it all? What were they about to steal? And why was that code vaguely familiar? With all these thoughts spinning around in her head, Kaz finally drifted off to sleep.

The next morning, Matt had a bright idea. "Let's ask Hal Gough for some help," he said. "After all, he knows more than we do about the tunnels."

They drove to Hal's house. He was surprised to see them, but said he'd try to help.

"You already seem to know as much as I do," he began. "But –"

Hal never had a chance to finish. Suddenly everything started happening at once.

First there was a ring at the front doorbell. It was Eduardo Jones. "My warehouse has been raided!" he cried as soon as he walked through the door. "When I got in this morning, whole *piles* of boxes had been taken."

All kinds of things were taken – fireworks, fake bombs, smoke canisters...

Uh oh, wrong again, thought Kaz. From the sound of it, Eduardo was innocent – and had nothing to do with the heavily disguised men at his warehouse.

Before they could find out more, there was a hammering on the door. This time it was a breathless Constanza Smith.

"Have you heard the news?" she gasped. "Someone is *blowing up* the Royal Fort! Smoke is pouring from the building this very minute! The place will burn to the ground in no time! Really, this city is a disaster area! First the Traitor's Knot was stolen, then someone committed an *outrage* at the Governor's Mansion. And now *this*!" She paused for breath.

"This must be the work of the thieves," said Kaz decisively. "Come on Matt, I've got a feeling we're about to really prove our worth!" In moments they were on their way to the Royal Fort...

Panic!

Matt and Kaz sprinted into the square and skidded to a halt, staring in amazement. Huge clouds of smoke, bangs, flashes, sparks – the Fort seemed to be having its very own firework extravaganza! Given what Eduardo had said he'd lost, it was a fair bet most of his stock was going up in flames before their very eyes.

The message they'd found on the Seamist was beginning to make sense, thought Kaz. Someone had targeted this building, for sure! And there was enough chaos and confusion here to distract an army of guards... guards... vaults... wait a minute...

"Quick!" said Kaz, thinking back to their case file and the pile of junk mail, "I've just worked out what the villains are planning to steal!"

What?

The Villains Strike

The Allegro Crown Jewels! The city's most priceless treasures!

"We've got to tell someone!" cried Kaz. They rushed over to a group of security guards to try and explain.

The guards weren't very impressed at first – not surprising really, given Kaz and Matt's appearance – but at last, after an exchange of radio messages, they set off at a run, with Kaz and Matt behind them.

They headed for a side entrance, then raced along darkened corridors, until they reached the vault where the Crown Jewels were kept.

One guard keyed in the code to open the door, and then gasped. The vault was empty!

With guards panicking all around them, Kaz and Matt headed straight into the vault.

"There – look," shouted Matt above the din, pointing at a gaping hole in the wall. "A doorway!"

Kaz was not surprised to find that it led directly into the network of underground tunnels.

Matt and Kaz plunged into the tunnels, which led off in different directions. Which way had the thieves gone? As Kaz reached the top of a flight of steps, she spotted a scrap of paper on the ground.

Snatching it up, she guessed it had been dropped by one of the escaping gang of villains.

Kaz and Matt quickly skimmed through the note.

At last the identity of the gang leader was clear. What was more, the city map and Traitor's Knot would tell them where the villains were heading.

Who is the leader? Where will the villains leave the tunnels?

The modern map will tell us what the building's called.

Gus:
Crimebusters are off my trail. Staging my kidnapping was a great idea! Now we can get on with the master plan. I have been into the old tunnels. Everything is perfect. After taking the jewels, we'll come out through the tunnel entrance nearest to the Fort. More instructions soon.

Getaway

Sally Malloney! Their first ever suspect... so she'd been guilty all along! Matt and Kaz raced back out of the tunnels, and set off above ground for the Grapevine café. But would they be in time to intercept the villains?

The café was right next to the Royal Fort, and the whole area was still in turmoil.

"Follow me," ordered Kaz, scrambling up onto a high-up balcony to get a better view.

"The thieves can't be far away," she cried, as Matt joined her. They scanned the crowded street below, trying to spot Sally and her gang.

Suddenly, Kaz let out a yell of triumph. "They're over there!" she shouted down to the guards. "Catch them!"

Can you spot the villains?

41

The Aftermath

Over the next few days, Kaz and Matt read all about their exploits in the papers, and got loads of letters, including one from Sally herself! You never know, thought Kaz, maybe we haven't seen the last of her yet!

Last night, intrepid investigators, Kaz Smiley and Matt Drake returned the Allegro Crown Jewels to the Royal Fort. Meanwhile, it was revealed that the building was unharmed by yesterday's events. The conspirators used theatrical smoke and other special effects to create the illusion of an explosion.

...also emerged ...y Malloney

...her accomplices were behind a string of other crimes.

Police have just revealed that Sally was working for the unscrupulous art collector, Jack Smithers. He met Sally Malloney at the Singing Kettle café last Thu...

Dear Crimebusters – or should that be Grimebusters? No doubt you're feeling very pleased with yourselves. But if Gus hadn't dropped that message in the tunnels you'd never have suspected me. You really went for the kidnapping story, didn't you? Not to mention the fake coded message! No, you weren't that clever – just lucky! See you again
– I promise!

YOU ARE INVITED TO THE OPENING NIGHT
OF A NEW OPERA
THE PHANTOM CONSPIRACY
STARRING WORLD-FAMOUS SOPRANO
CONSTANZA SMITH
AUGUST 29TH 8:00PM

Do hope you can both come – after all, it was the Phantom Conspiracy that made you suspect me of terrible deeds! Thank you for everything – Constanza.

All three members of the Crown Jewels Conspiracy were taken to Allegro Central police station following their arrest outside the Royal Fort. Sally Malloney, the cunning and devious ...

Dear Crimebusters,
Thank you for your splendid detective work! The whole city is grateful to you.
I was myself one of the few people who knew about the old tunnels – my old friend Annabelle Lotte wrote to me to tell me all about them – but I never dreamed they'd be used for a criminal plot!
Thank you once again –
Thomas Maverick
Governor of Allegro.

Dear Kaz,
Thought you might like to know I've inherited a fortune from my fourth cousin twice removed, so I'm not coming back! The newspapers here are full of your exploits, by the way – well done! However did you get into detecting? Anyway, I've decided to give you Grimebusters – maybe you could turn it into a detective agency! How's that for a ... idea?

love,
Mona

Clues

Pages 6-7

Look back to pages 4 and 5. Read all the notices!

Pages 8-9

Can you figure out how the pieces fit together?

Pages 10-11

Remember the message on page 9. How many of the suspects live on the same road as a café?

Pages 12-13

Five letters have been replaced by numbers.

Pages 14-15

Think carefully about the coded message on page 13.

Pages 16-17

Can you find the address of Miscellany antiques? Now check the suspects' addresses.

Pages 18-19

Remember the strange canisters found at the Governor's Mansion? Where could they have come from?

Pages 20-21

Remember where Sally lives?

Pages 22-23

Try each starting point in turn.

Pages 24-25

Try ignoring the spaces.

Pages 26-27

Look at the message on page 25.

Pages 30-31

Have you heard of the Aurora before?

Pages 32-33

Five letters have been replaced by numbers again. Which ones this time?

Pages 36-37

The message on page 33 says the villains' target is in vaults somewhere. Valuable things are kept in vaults – look back at papers on pages 11 and 19!

Pages 38-39

Remember Hal's diary on page 29. This should help you find the tunnel entrances. Use the modern map on page 21 to name the building where the thieves are heading.

Pages 40-41

They've hitched a ride.

Answers

Pages 6-7

Constanza Smith says that the leaflet was delivered 'last week'. It is now August 4, so the leaflet was delivered in July. Mary's notice on page 4, says that all leaflets delivered in July had a misprint, and came from box 4. You can see a sample leaflet stuck on this box at the bottom of page 5. It reads:

IF THERE'S DIRTY
WORK AROUND CALL
CRIMEBUSTERS
234 - 487 - 34
31 BACK STREET

Grimebusters has become Crimebusters! Kaz has been called in as a detective, to find the thief of the Traitor's Knot.

Pages 8-9

The pieces of paper fit together as shown, to reveal this message:

Wednesday 4th
Need to discuss latest developments Have you planned final swoop yet? Meet me tomorrow morning at ten to make arrangements for the handover. I'll be at the café at the end of your road.
Please be prompt.

Pages 10-11

Looking at the phone book entries and the page from the guide to Allegro, Kaz realizes that only one suspect lives on the same road as a café. It is Sally Malloney. The meeting place is the Singing Kettle café.

Pages 12-13

The vowels have been replaced by numbers. A is now 2, E is 3, I is 4, O is 5 and U is 6.
The message says: OPERATION SMOKESCREEN BEGINS AT 1:00 PM. MAP IN CABINET AT X. USE AGREED DISGUISE.

Pages 14-15

Everything fits in with Sally's coded instructions on page 13. The mansion is clouded in smoke, it's not long after 1:00 pm, and the running man Matt has noticed is holding a piece of paper that could well be a map. What's more, he is dressed as a fireman, but isn't behaving like one – is this the 'agreed disguise'?

Pages 16-17

The pieces of paper on pages 10 and 11 show that Annabelle Lotte has the same address as Miscellany antiques. She is the owner – so she wrote the note!

Pages 18-19

Eduardo Jones is clearly implicated here. The smoke canister pictured in the ad for Eduardo's Theatrical Supplies is the same as the ones on the floor at Marvello Mansion and in the man's hand at the Governor's Mansion. And there's no other Eduardo involved – the address is the same as his address in the phone book (page 10).

Pages 20-21

The route is shown here in red. It leads to the Hotel Grande.

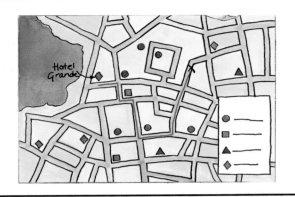

Pages 22-23

The safe, unbroken route is shown here in red.

Pages 24-25

To decode the message, Kaz and Matt first take out all punctuation marks and word spaces. Then they put capital letters in the right places, and add punctuation and spaces once again. This is what it says:

Meet me at the train station at eleven am on August sixth at the snack bar next to a chocolate shop. It is in the same row as one of the bookshops, but is not directly opposite a florist. I will be wearing my usual brown hat.

Pages 26-27

Using the station plan, and the message on page 25, Kaz and Matt work out that the meeting will take place at this snack bar.

They spot two familiar figures sitting at one of the tables. They are Hal Gough and Annabelle Lotte, circled in red.

Pages 30-31

Kaz remembers that the Aurora is the name of the houseboat she cleaned on Wednesday. In the picture on page 4, you can see that one of the other boats at Orlando Wharf is called the Aleppo. Between the Aleppo and the Aurora is the Seamist.

This must be the villains' 'safe place'.

Pages 32-33

The letters L, N, R, S and T have been replaced by numbers. L is now 2, N is 3, R is 4, S is 5 and T is 6.

The message says: HERE IS THE FINAL PLAN: WE WILL CREATE CHAOS AND CONFUSION AT TARGET BUILDING AT 11:00. THIS WILL DISTRACT GUARDS WHO KEEP VAULTS UNDER CONSTANT SURVEILLANCE. THEN WE'LL ENTER VAULTS THROUGH TUNNELS AND CARRY OUT THEFT.

Pages 36-37

From the message on page 33, Kaz knows that the villains are intending to steal something from the vaults of a 'target building'. The leaflets on pages 11 and 19 reveal that the Allegro Crown Jewels are kept in the vaults of the Royal Fort. These are the most valuable treasures in the whole city – they must be what the villains are after!

Pages 38-39

The reference to staging a kidnap is an instant giveaway: Sally Malloney has to be guilty!

To figure out where she and her gang are heading, Kaz and Matt think back to Hal's diary (page 29). There are four symbols on the old map that match symbols on the Traitor's Knot. They show the sites of buildings with tunnel entrances.
The Royal Fort has the ☆ symbol on the old map. The nearest entrance to it is in the building with the ⊛ symbol. From the modern map, Kaz and Matt can name this as The Grapevine café.

Pages 40-41

Sally Malloney and her accomplices are riding on a fire engine – appropriate really, given the disguises they've used in the past. They are circled in red.

First published in 1997 by Usborne Publishing Ltd, Usborne House, 83-85 Saffron Hill, London EC1N 8RT, England.
Copyright © 1997 Usborne Publishing Ltd.
The name Usborne and the device are Trade Marks of Usborne Publishing Ltd. All rights reserved.